I0460929

THE SHADOW OF THE VULTURE

BY

ROBERT E. HOWARD

Copyright © 2013 Read Books Ltd.
This book is copyright and may not be
reproduced or copied in any way without
the express permission of the publisher in writing

British Library Cataloguing-in-Publication Data
A catalogue record for this book is available from the
British Library

Contents

Robert E. Howard

Robert Ervin Howard was born in Peaster, Texas in 1906. During his youth, his family moved between a variety of Texan boomtowns, and Howard – a bookish and somewhat introverted child – was steeped in the violent myths and legends of the Old South. Although he loved reading and learning, Howard developed a distinctly Texan, hardboiled outlook on the world. He became a passionate fan of boxing, taking it up at an amateur level, and from the age of nine began to write adventure tales of semi-historical bloodshed. In 1919, when Howard was thirteen, his family moved to the Central Texas hamlet of Cross Plains, where he would stay for the rest of his life.

At fifteen Howard began to read the pulp magazines of the day, and to write more seriously. The December 1922 issue of his high school newspaper featured two of his stories, 'Golden Hope Christmas' and 'West is West'. In 1924 he sold his first piece – a short caveman tale titled 'Spear and Fang' – for $16 to the not-yet-famous *Weird Tales* magazine. He published with the magazine regularly over the next few years. 1929 was a breakout year for Howard, in that the 23-year-old writer began to sell to other magazines, such as *Ghost Stories* and *Argosy*, both of whom had previously sent him hundreds of rejection slips. In 1930, he began a correspondence with weird fiction master H. P. Lovecraft which ran up to his death six years later, and is regarded as one of the great correspondence cycles in all of fantasy literature.

It was partly due to Lovecraft's encouragement that Howard created his most famous character, Conan the Cimmerian. Conan – a barbarian-turned-King during the Hyborian Age, a mythical period of some 12,000 years ago – featured in seventeen *Weird Tales* stories between 1933 and 1936, and is now regarded as having spawned the 'sword and sorcery' genre, making Howard's influence on fantasy literature comparable to that of J. R. R. Tolkien's. The Conan stories have since been adapted many times, most famously in the series of films starring Arnold Schwarzenegger.

Howard was enjoying an all-time high in sales by the beginning of 1936, but he was also deeply upset by the ill health of his mother, who had fallen into a coma. On the morning of June 11, 1936, he asked an attending nurse whether she would ever recover, and the nurse replied negatively. Howard walked to his car, parked outside the family home in Cross Plains, and shot himself. He died eight hours later, aged just thirty.

CHAPTER 1

"Are the dogs dressed and gorged?"

"Aye, Protector of the Faithful."

"Then let them crawl into the Presence."

So they brought the envoys, pallid from months of imprisonment, before the canopied throne of Suleyman the Magnificent, Sultan of Turkey, and the mightiest monarch in an age of mighty monarchs. Under the great purple dome of the royal chamber gleamed the throne before which the world trembled--gold-paneled, pearl-inlaid. An emperor's wealth in gems was sewn into the silken canopy from which depended a shimmering string of pearls ending a frieze of emeralds which hung like a halo of glory above Suleyman's head. Yet the splendor of the throne was paled by the glitter of the figure upon it, bedecked in jewels, the aigrette feather rising above the diamonded white turban. About the throne stood his nine viziers, in attitudes of humility, and warriors of the imperial bodyguard ranged the dais--Solaks in armor, black and white and scarlet plumes nodding above the gilded helmets.

The envoys from Austria were properly impressed--the more so as they had had nine weary months for reflection in the grim Castle of the Seven Towers that overlooks the Sea of Marmora. The head of the embassy choked down his choler and cloaked his resentment in a semblance of submission--a strange cloak on the shoulders of Habordansky, general of Ferdinand, Archduke of Austria. His rugged head bristled incongruously from the flaming silk robes presented him by the contemptuous Sultan, as he was brought before the throne, his arms gripped fast by stalwart Janizaries. Thus were foreign envoys presented to the sultans, ever since that red day by Kossova when Milosh Kabilovitch, knight of slaughtered Serbia, had slain the conqueror Murad with a hidden dagger.

The Grand Turk regarded Habordansky with scant favor. Suleyman was a tall, slender man, with a thin down-curving nose and a thin straight mouth, the resolution of which his drooping mustachios did not soften. His narrow outward-curving chin was shaven. The only suggestion of weakness was in the slender, remarkably long neck, but that suggestion was belied by the hard lines of the slender figure, the glitter of the dark eyes. There was more than a suggestion of the Tatar about him--rightly so, since he was no more the son of Selim the Grim, than of Hafsza Khatun, princess of Crimea. Born to the purple, heir to the mightiest military power in the world, he was crested with authority and cloaked in pride that recognized no peer beneath the gods.

Under his eagle gaze old Habordansky bent his head to hide the sullen rage in his eyes. Nine months before, the general had come to Stamboul representing his master, the

4

Archduke, with proposals for truce and the disposition of the iron crown of Hungary, torn from the dead king Louis' head on the bloody field of Mohacz, where the Grand Turk's armies opened the road to Europe. There had been another emissary before him--Jerome Lasczky, the Polish count palatine. Habordansky, with the bluntness of his breed, had claimed the Hungarian crown for his master, rousing Suleyman's ire. Lasczky had, like a suppliant, asked on his bended knees that crown for his countrymen at Mohacz.

To Lasczky had been given honor, gold and promises of patronage, for which he had paid with pledges abhorrent even to his avaricious soul--selling his ally's subjects into slavery, and opening the road through the subject territory to the very heart of Christendom.

All this was made known to Habordansky, frothing with fury in the prison to which the arrogant resentment of the Sultan had assigned him. Now Suleyman looked contemptuously at the staunch old general, and dispensed with the usual formality of speaking through the mouthpiece of the Grand Vizier. A royal Turk would not deign to admit knowledge of any Frankish tongue, but Habordansky understood Turki. The Sultan's remarks were brief and without preamble.

"Say to your master that I now make ready to visit him in his own lands, and that if he fails to meet me at Mohacz or at Pesth, I will meet him beneath the walls of Vienna."

Habordansky bowed, not trusting himself to speak. At a scornful wave of the imperial hand, an officer of the court came forward and bestowed upon the general a small gilded bag containing two hundred ducats. Each member of his retinue, waiting patiently at the other end of the chamber, under the spears of the Janizaries, was likewise so guerdoned. Habordansky mumbled thanks, his knotty hands clenched about the gift with unnecessary vigor. The Sultan grinned thinly, well aware that the ambassador would have hurled the coins into his face, had he dared. He half-lifted his hand, in token of dismissal, then paused, his eyes resting on the group of men who composed the general's suite--or rather, on one of these men. This man was the tallest in the room, strongly built, wearing his Turkish gift-garments clumsily. At a gesture from the Sultan he was brought forward in the grasp of the soldiers.

Suleyman stared at him narrowly. The Turkish vest and voluminous khalat could not conceal the lines of massive strength. His tawny hair was close-cropped, his sweeping yellow mustaches drooping below a stubborn chin. His blue eyes seemed strangely clouded; it was as if the man slept on his feet, with his eyes open.

"Do you speak Turki?" The Sultan did the fellow the stupendous honor of addressing him directly. Through all the pomp of the Ottoman court there remained in the Sultan some of the simplicity of Tatar ancestors.

"Yes, your majesty," answered the Frank.

"Who are you?"

"Men name me Gottfried von Kalmbach."

Suleyman scowled and unconsciously his fingers wandered to his shoulder, where, under his silken robes, he could feel the outlines of an old scar.

"I do not forget faces. Somewhere I have seen yours--under circumstances that etched it into the back of my mind. But I am unable to recall those circumstances."

"I was at Rhodes," offered the German.

"Many men were at Rhodes," snapped Suleyman.

"Aye." agreed von Kalmbach tranquilly. "De l'Isle Adam was there."

Suleyman stiffened and his eyes glittered at the name of the Grand Master of the Knights of Saint John, whose desperate defense of Rhodes had cost the Turk sixty thousand men. He decided, however, that the Frank was not clever enough for the remark to carry any subtle thrust, and dismissed the embassy with a wave. The envoys were backed out of the Presence and the incident was closed. The Franks would be escorted out of Stamboul, and to the nearest boundaries of the empire. The Turk's warning would be carried posthaste to the Archduke, and soon on the heels of that warning would come the armies of the Sublime Porte. Suleyman's officers knew that the Grand Turk had more in mind than merely establishing his puppet Zapolya on the conquered Hungarian throne. Suleyman's ambitions embraced all Europe--that stubborn Frankistan which had for centuries sporadically poured forth hordes chanting and pillaging into the East, whose illogical and wayward peoples had again and again seemed ripe for Moslem conquest, yet who had always emerged, if not victorious, at least unconquered.

It was the evening of the morning on which the Austrian emissaries departed that Suleyman, brooding on his throne, raised his lean head and beckoned his Grand Vizier Ibrahim, who approached with confidence. The Grand Vizier was always sure of his master's approbation; was he not cup-companion and boyhood comrade of the Sultan? Ibrahim had but one rival in his master's favor--the red-haired Russian girl, Khurrem the Joyous, whom Europe knew as Roxelana, whom slavers had dragged from her father's house in Rogatino to be the Sultan's harim favorite.

"I remember the infidel at last," said Suleyman. "Do you recall the first charge of the knights at Mohacz?"

Ibrahim winced slightly at the allusion.

"Oh, Protector of the Pitiful, is it likely that I should forget an occasion on which the divine blood of my master was spilt by an unbeliever?"

"Then you remember that thirty-two knights, the paladins of the Nazarenes, drove headlong into our array, each having pledged his life to cut down our person. By

Allah, they rode like men riding to a wedding, their great horses and long lances overthrowing all who opposed them, and their plate-armor turned the finest steel. Yet they fell as the firelocks spoke until only three were left in the saddle--the knight Marczali and two companions. These paladins cut down my Solaks like ripe grain, but Marczali and one of his companions fell--almost at my feet.

"Yet one knight remained, though his vizored helmet had been torn from his head and blood started from every joint in his armor. He rode full at me, swinging his great two-handed sword, and I swear by the beard of the Prophet, death was so nigh me that I felt the burning breath of Azrael on my neck!

"His sword flashed like lightning in the sky, and glancing from my casque, whereby I was half-stunned so that blood gushed from my nose, rent the mail on my shoulder and gave me this wound, which irks me yet when the rains come. The Janizaries who swarmed around him cut the hocks of his horse, which brought him to earth as it went down, and the remnants of my Solaks bore me back out of the melee. Then the Hungarian host came on, and I saw not what became of the knight. But today I saw him again."

Ibrahim started with an exclamation of incredulity.

"Nay, I could not mistake those blue eyes. How it is I know not, but the knight that wounded me at Mohacz was this German, Gottfried von Kalmbach."

"But, Defender of the Faith," protested Ibrahim, "the heads of those dog-knights were heaped before thy royal pavilion--"

"And I counted them and said nothing at the time, lest men think I held thee in blame," answered Suleyman. "There were but thirty-one. Most were so mutilated I could tell little of the features. But somehow the infidel escaped, who gave me this blow. I love brave men, but our blood is not so common that an unbeliever may with impunity spill it on the ground for the dogs to lap up. See ye to it."

Ibrahim salaamed deeply and withdrew. He made his way through broad corridors to a blue-tiled chamber whose gold-arched windows looked out on broad galleries, shaded by cypress and plane-trees, and cooled by the spray of silvery fountains. There at his summons came one Yaruk Khan, a Crim Tatar, a slant-eyed impassive figure in harness of lacquered leather and burnished bronze.

"Dog-brother," said the Vizier, "did thy koumiss-clouded gaze mark the tall German lord who served the emir Habordansky--the lord whose hair is tawny as a lion's mane?"

"Aye, noyon' he who is called Gombuk."

"The same. Take a chambul of thy dog-brothers and go after the Franks. Bring back this man and thou shalt be rewarded. The persons of envoys are sacred, but this matter is not official," he added cynically.

10

"To hear is to obey!" With a salaam as profound as that accorded to the Sultan himself, Yaruk Khan backed out of the presence of the second man of the empire.

He returned some days later, dusty, travel-stained, and without his prey. On him Ibrahim bent an eye full of menace, and the Tatar prostrated himself before the silken cushions on which the Grand Vizier sat, in the blue chamber with the gold-arched windows.

"Great khan, let not thine anger consume thy slave. The fault was not mine, by the beard of the Prophet."

"Squat on thy mangy haunches and bay out the tale," ordered Ibrahim considerately.

"Thus it was, my lord," began Yaruk Khan. "I rode swiftly, and though the Franks and their escort had a long start, and pushed on through the night without halting, I came up with them the next midday. But lo, Gombuk was not among them, and when I inquired after him, the paladin Habordansky replied only with many great oaths, like to the roaring of a cannon. So I spoke with various of the escort who understood the speech of these infidels, and learned what had come to pass. Yet I would have my lord remember that I only repeat the words of the Spahis of the escort, who are men without honor and lie like--"

"Like a Tatar," said Ibrahim.

Yaruk Khan acknowledged the compliment with a wide dog-like grin, and continued. "This they told me. At

11

dawn Gombuk drew horse away from the rest, and the emir Habordansky demanded of him the reason. Then Gombuk laughed in the manner of the Franks--huh! huh! huh!--so. And Gombuk said, 'The devil of good your service has done me, so I cool my heels for nine months in a Turkish prison. Suleyman has given us safe conduct over the border and I am not compelled to ride with you.' 'You dog,' said the emir, 'there is war in the wind and the Archduke has need of your sword.' 'Devil eat the Archduke,' answered Gombuk; 'Zapolya is a dog because he stood aside at Mohacz, and let us, his comrades, be cut to pieces, but Ferdinand is a dog too. When I am penniless I sell him my sword. Now I have two hundred ducats and these robes which I can sell to any Jew for a handful of silver, and may the devil bite me if I draw sword for any man while I have a penny left. I'm for the nearest Christian tavern, and you and the Archduke may go to the devil.' Then the emir cursed him with many great curses, and Gombuk rode away laughing, huh! huh! huh!, and singing a song about a cockroach named--"

"Enough!" Ibrahim's features were dark with rage. He plucked savagely at his beard, reflecting that in the allusion to Mohacz, von Kalmbach had practically clinched Suleyman's suspicion. That matter of thirty-one heads when there should have been thirty-two was something no Turkish sultan would be likely to overlook. Officials had lost positions and their own heads over more trivial matters. The manner in which

Suleyman had acted showed his almost incredible fondness and consideration for his Grand Vizier, but Ibrahim, vain though he was, was shrewd and wished no slightest shadow to come between him and his sovereign.

"Could you not have tracked him down, dog?" he demanded.

"By Allah," swore the uneasy Tatar, "he must have ridden on the wind. He crossed the border hours ahead of me, and I followed him as far as I dared--"

"Enough of excuses," interrupted Ibrahim. "Send Mikhal Oglu to me."

The Tatar departed thankfully. Ibrahim was not tolerant of failure in any man.

The Grand Vizier brooded on his silken cushions until the shadow of a pair of vulture wings fell across the marble-tiled floor, and the lean figure he had summoned bowed before him. The man whose very name was a shuddering watchword of horror to all western Asia was soft-spoken and moved with the mincing ease of a cat, but the stark evil of his soul showed in his dark countenance, gleamed in his narrow slit eyes. He was the chief of the Akinji, those wild riders whose raids spread fear and desolation throughout all lands beyond the Grand Turk's borders. He stood in full armor, a jeweled helmet on his narrow head, the wide vulture wings made fast to the shoulders of his gilded chain-mail hauberk. Those wings spread wide in the wind when he rode, and under their pinions lay the shadows of death and destruction. It was Suleyman's scimitar-tip, the most noted slayer of a nation of slayers, who stood before the Grand Vizier.

"Soon you will precede the hosts of our master into the lands of the infidel," said Ibrahim. "It will be your order, as always, to strike and spare not. You will waste the fields and the vineyards of the Caphars, you will burn their villages, you will strike down their men with arrows, and lead away their wenches captive. Lands beyond our line of march will cry out beneath your heel."

"That is good hearing, Favored of Allah," answered Mikhal Oglu in his soft courteous voice.

"Yet there is an order within the order," continued Ibrahim, fixing a piercing eye on the Akinji. "You know the German, von Kalmbach?"

"Aye--Gombuk as the Tatars call him."

"So. This is my command--whoever fights or flees, lives or dies--this man must not live. Search him out wherever he lies, though the hunt carry you to the very banks of the Rhine. When you bring me his head, your reward shall be thrice its weight in gold."

"To hear is to obey, my lord. Men say he is the vagabond son of a noble German family, whose ruin has been wine and women. They say he was once a Knight of Saint John, until cast forth for guzzling and--"

"Yet do not underrate him," answered Ibrahim grimly. "Sot he may be, but if he rode with Marczali, he is not to be despised. See thou to it!"

"There is no den where he can hide from me, oh Favored of Allah," declared Mikhal Oglu, "no night dark enough to conceal him, no forest thick enough. If I bring you not his head, I give him leave to send you mine."

"Enough!" Ibrahim grinned and tugged at his beard, well pleased. "You have my leave to go."

The sinister vulture-winged figure went springily and silently from the blue chamber, nor could Ibrahim guess that he was taking the first steps in a feud which should spread over years and far lands, swirling in dark tides to draw in thrones and kingdoms and red-haired women more beautiful than the flames of hell.

CHAPTER 2

In a small thatched hut in a village not far from the Danube, lusty snores resounded where a figure reclined in state on a ragged cloak thrown over a heap of straw. It was the paladin Gottfried von Kalmbach who slept the sleep of innocence and ale. The velvet vest, voluminous silken trousers, khalat and shagreen boots, gifts from a contemptuous sultan, were nowhere in evidence. The paladin was clad in worn leather and rusty mail. Hands tugged at him, breaking his sleep, and he swore drowsily.

"Wake up, my lord! Oh, wake, good knight--good pig--good dog-soul--will you wake, then?"

"Fill my flagon, host," mumbled the slumberer. "Who?--what? May the dogs bite you, Ivga! I've not another asper--not a penny. Go off like a good lass and let me sleep."

The girl renewed her tugging and shaking.

"Oh dolt! Rise! Gird on your spit! There are happenings forward!"

"Ivga," muttered Gottfried, pulling away from her attack, "take my burganet to the Jew. He'll give you enough for it to get drunk again."

"Fool!" she cried in despair. "It isn't money I want! The whole east is aflame, and none knows the reason thereof!"

"Has the rain ceased?" asked von Kalmbach, taking some interest in the proceedings at last.

"The rain ceased hours ago. You can only hear the drip from the thatch. Put on your sword and come out into the street. The men of the village are all drunk on your last silver, and the women know not what to think or do. Ah!"

The exclamation was broken from her by the sudden upleaping of a weird illumination which shone through the crevices of the hut. The German got unsteadily to his feet, quickly girt on the great two-handed sword and stuck his dented burganet on his cropped locks. Then he followed the girl into the straggling street. She was a slender young thing, barefooted, clad only in a short tunic-like garment, through the wide rents of which gleamed generous expanses of white flesh.

There seemed no life or movement in the village. Nowhere showed a light. Water dripped steadily from the eaves of the thatched roofs. Puddles in the muddy streets gleamed black. Wind sighed and moaned eerily through the black sodden branches of the trees which pressed in bulwarks of darkness about the little village, and in the southeast, towering higher into the leaden sky, rose the lurid crimson glow that set the dank clouds to smoldering. The girl Ivga cringed close to the tall German, whimpering.

"I'll tell you what it is, my girl," said he, scanning the glow. "It's Suleyman's devils. They've crossed the river and they're burning the villages. Aye, I've seen glares like that in the sky before. I've expected him before now, but these cursed rains we've had for weeks must have held him back. Aye, it's the Akinji, right enough, and they won't stop this side of Vienna. Look you, my girl, go quickly and quietly to the stable behind the hut and bring me my gray stallion. We'll slip out like mice from between the devil's fingers. The stallion will carry us both, easily."

"But the people of the village!" she sobbed, wringing her hands.

"Eh, well," he said, "God rest them; the men have drunk my ale valiantly and the women have been kind--but horns of Satan, girl, the gray nag won't carry a whole village!"

"Go you!" she returned. "I'll stay and die with my people!"

"The Turks won't kill you," he answered. "They'll sell you to a fat old Stamboul merchant who'll beat you. I won't stay to be cut open, and neither shall you--"

A terrible scream from the girl cut him short and he wheeled at the awful terror in her flaring eyes. Even as he did so, a hut at the lower end of the village sprang into flames, the sodden material burning slowly. A medley of screams and maddened yells followed the cry of the girl. In the sluggish light figures danced and capered wildly. Gottfried, straining his eyes in the shadows, saw shapes swarming over the low mud wall which drunkenness and negligence had left unguarded.

"Damnation!" he muttered. "The accursed ones have ridden ahead of their fire. They've stolen on the village in the dark--come on, girl!"

But even as he caught her white wrist to drag her away, and she screamed and fought against him like a wild thing, mad with fear, the mud wall crashed at the point nearest them. It crumpled under the impact of a score of horses, and into the doomed village reined the riders, distinct in the growing light. Huts were flaring up on all hands, screams rising to the dripping clouds as the invaders dragged shrieking women and drunken men from their hovels and cut their throats. Gottfried saw the lean figures of the horsemen, the firelight gleaming on their burnished steel; he saw the vulture wings on the shoulders of the foremost. Even as he recognized Mikhal Oglu, he saw the chief stiffen and point.

"At him, dogs!" yelled the Akinji, his voice no longer soft, but strident as the rasp of a drawn saber. "It is Gombuk! Five hundred aspers to the man who brings me his head!"

With a curse von Kalmbach bounded for the shadows of the nearest hut, dragging the screaming girl with him. Even as he leaped he heard the twang of bowstrings, and the girl sobbed and went limp in his grasp. She sank down at his feet, and in the lurid glare he saw the feathered end of an arrow quivering under her heart. With a low rumble he turned toward his assailants as a fierce bear turns at bay. An instant he stood, head out-thrust truculently, sword gripped in both hands; then, as a bear gives back from the onset of the hunters, he turned and fled about the hut, arrows whistling about him and glancing from the rings of his mail. There were no shots; the ride through that dripping forest had dampened the powder-flasks of the raiders.

Von Kalmbach quartered about the back of the hut, mindful of the fierce yells behind him, and gained the shed behind the hut he had occupied, wherein he stabled his gray stallion. Even as he reached the door, someone snarled like a panther in the semi-dark and cut viciously at him. He parried the stroke with the lifted sword and struck back with all the power of his broad shoulders. The great blade glanced stunningly from the Akinji's polished helmet and rent through the mail links of his hauberk, tearing arm from shoulder. The Muhammadan sank down with a groan, and the German sprang over his prostrate form. The gray stallion, wild with fear and excitement, neighed shrilly and reared as his master sprang on his back. No time for saddle or bridle. Gottfried dug his heels into the quivering flanks and the great steed shot through the door like a thunderbolt, knocking men right and left like tenpins. Across the firelit open space between the burning huts he raced, clearing crumpled corpses in his stride, splashing his rider from heel to head as he thrashed through the puddles.

The Akinji made after the flying rider, loosing their shafts and giving tongue like hounds. Those mounted spurred after him, while those who had entered the village on foot ran through the broken wall for their horses.

Arrows flickered about Gottfried's head as he put his steed at the only point open to him--the unbroken western wall. It was touch and go, for the footing was tricky and treacherous and never had the gray stallion attempted such a leap. Gottfried held his breath as he felt the great body beneath him gathering and tensing in full flight for the desperate effort; then with a volcanic heave of mighty thews the stallion rose in the air and cleared the barrier with scarce an inch to spare. The pursuers yelled in amazement and fury, and reined back. Born horsemen though they were, they dared not attempt that breakneck leap. They lost time seeking gates and breaks in the wall, and when they finally emerged from the village, the black, dank, whispering, dripping forest had swallowed up their prey.

Mikhal Oglu swore like a fiend and leaving his lieutenant Othman in charge with instructions to leave no living human being in the village, he pressed on after the fugitive, following the trail, by torches, in the muddy mold, and swearing to run him down, if the road led under the very walls of Vienna.

CHAPTER 3

Allah did not will it that Mikhal Oglu should take Gottfried von Kalmbach's head in the dark, dripping forest. He knew the country better than they, and in spite of their zeal, they lost his trail in the darkness. Dawn found Gottfried riding through terror-stricken farmlands, with the flame of a burning world lighting the east and south. The country was thronged with fugitives, staggering under pitiful loads of household goods, driving bellowing cattle, like people fleeing the end of the world. The torrential rains that had offered false promise of security had not long stayed the march of the Grand Turk.

With a quarter-million followers he was ravaging the eastern marches of Christendom. While Gottfried had loitered in the taverns of isolated villages, drinking up the Sultan's bounty, Pesth and Buda had fallen, the German soldiers of the latter having been slaughtered by the Janizaries, after promises of safety sworn by Suleyman, whom men named the Generous.

While Ferdinand and the nobles and bishops squabbled at the Diet of Spires, the elements alone seemed to war for Christendom. Rain fell in torrents, and through the floods that changed plains and forest-bed to dank morasses, the Turks struggled grimly. They drowned in raging rivers, and lost great stores of ammunition, ordnance and supplies when boats capsized, bridges gave way, and wagons mired. But on they came, driven by the implacable will of Suleyman, and now in September, 1529, over the ruins of Hungary, the Turk swept on Europe, with the Akinji--the Sackmen---ravaging the land like the drift ahead of a storm.

This in part Gottfried learned from the fugitives as he pushed his weary stallion toward the city which was the only sanctuary for the panting thousands. Behind him the skies flamed red and the screams of butchered victims came dimly down the wind to his ears. Sometimes he could even make out the swarming black masses of wild horsemen. The wings of the vulture beat horrifically over that butchered land and the shadows of those great wings fell across all Europe. Again the destroyer was riding out of the blue mysterious East as his brothers had ridden before him--Attila--Subotai--Bayazid--Muhammad the Conqueror. But never before had such a storm risen against the West.

Before the waving vulture wings the road thronged with wailing fugitives; behind them it ran red and silent, strewn with mangled shapes that cried no more. The killers were not a half-hour behind him when Gottfried von Kalmbach rode his reeling stallion through the gates of Vienna. The people on the walls had heard the wailing for hours, rising awfully on the wind, and now afar they saw the sun flicker on the points of lances as the horsemen rode in amongst the masses of fugitives toiling down from the hills into the plain which girdles the city. They saw the play of naked steel like sickles among ripe grain.

Von Kalmbach found the city in turmoil, the people swirling and screaming about Count Nikolas Salm, the seventy-year-old warhorse who commanded Vienna, and his aides, Roggendrof, Count Nikolas Zrinyi and Paul Bakics. Salm was working with frantic haste, leveling houses near the walls and using their material to brace the ramparts, which were old and unstable, nowhere more than six feet thick, and in many places crumbling and falling down. The outer palisade was so frail it bore the name of Stadtzaun--city hedge.

But under the lashing energy of Count Salm, a new wall twenty feet high was thrown up from the Stuben to the Karnthner Gate. Ditches interior to the old moat were dug, and ramparts erected from the drawbridge to the Salz Gate. Roofs were stripped of shingles, to lessen the chances of fire, and paving was ripped up to soften the impact of cannonballs.

The suburbs had been deserted, and now they were fired lest they give shelter to the besiegers. In the process, which was carried out in the very teeth of the oncoming Sackmen, conflagrations broke out in the city and added to the delirium. It was all hell and bedlam turned loose, and in the midst of it, five thousand wretched noncombatants, old men and women, and children, were ruthlessly driven from the gates to shift for themselves, and their screams, as the Akinjis swooped down, maddened the people within the walls. These hellions were arriving by thousands, topping the skylines, and sweeping down on the city in irregular squadrons, like vultures gathering about a dying camel. Within an hour after the first swarm had appeared, not one Christian remained alive outside the gates, except those bound by long ropes to the saddle-peaks of their captors and forced to run at full speed or be dragged to death. The wild riders swirled about the walls, yelling and loosing their shafts. Men on the towers recognized the dread Mikhal Oglu by the wings on his cuirass, and noted that he rode from one heap of dead to another, avidly scanning each corpse in turn, pausing to glare questioningly at the battlements.

Meanwhile, from the west, a band of German and Spanish troops cut their way through a cordon of Sackmen and marched into the streets to the accompaniment of frenzied cheers, Philip the Palgrave at their head.

Gottfried von Kalmbach leaned on his sword and watched them pass in their gleaming breastplates and plumed crested helmets, with long matchlocks on their shoulders and two-handed swords strapped to their steel-clad backs. He was a curious contrast in his rusty chain-mail, old-fashioned harness picked up here and there and slovenly pieced together--he seemed like a figure out of the past, rusty and tarnished, watching a newer, brighter generation go by. Yet Philip saluted him, with a glance of recognition, as the shining column swung past.

Von Kalmbach started toward the walls, where the gunners were firing frugally at the Akinji, who showed some disposition to climb upon the bastions on lariats thrown from their saddles. But on the way he heard that Salm was impressing nobles and soldiers in the task of digging moats and rearing new earthworks, and in great haste he took refuge in a tavern, where he bullied the host, a knock-kneed and apprehensive Wallachian, into giving him credit, and rapidly drank himself into a state where no one would have considered asking him to do work of any kind.

Shots, shouts and screams reached his ears, but he paid scant heed. He knew that the Akinji would strike and pass on, to ravage the country beyond. He learned from the tavern talk that Salm had 20,000 pikemen, 2,000 horsemen and 1,000 volunteer citizens to oppose Suleyman's hordes, together with seventy guns--cannons, demi-cannons and culverins. The news of the Turks' numbers numbed all hearts with dread--all but von Kalmbach's. He was a fatalist in his way. But he discovered a conscience in ale, and was presently brooding over the people the miserable Viennese had driven forth to perish. The more he drank the more melancholy he became, and maudlin tears dripped from the drooping ends of his mustaches.

At last he rose unsteadily and took up his great sword, muzzily intent on challenging Count Salm to a duel because of the matter. He bellowed down the timid importunities of the Wallachian and weaved out on the street. To his groggy sight the towers and spires cavorted crazily; people jostled him, knocking him aside as they ran about aimlessly. Philip the Palgrave strode by clanking in his armor, the keen dark faces of his Spaniards contrasting with the square, florid countenances of the Lanzknechts.

"Shame upon you, von Kalmbach!" said Philip sternly. "The Turk is upon us, and you keep your snout shoved in an ale-pot!"

"Whose snout is in what ale-pot?" demanded Gottfried, weaving in an erratic half-circle as he fumbled at his sword. "Devil bite you, Philip, I'll rap your pate for that--"

The Palgrave was already out of sight, and eventually Gottfried found himself on the Karnthner Tower, only vaguely aware of how he had got there. But what he saw sobered him suddenly. The Turk was indeed upon Vienna. The plain was covered with his tents, thirty thousand, some said, and swore that from the lofty spire of Saint Stephen's cathedral a man could not see their limits. Four hundred of his boats lay on the Danube, and Gottfried heard men cursing the Austrian fleet which lay helpless far upstream, because its sailors, long unpaid, refused to man the ships. He also heard that Salm had made no reply at all to Suleyman's demand to surrender.

Now, partly as a gesture, partly to awe the Caphar dogs, the Grand Turk's array was moving in orderly procession before the ancient walls before settling down to the business of the siege. The sight was enough to awe the stoutest. The low-swinging sun struck fire from polished helmet, jeweled saber-hilt and lance-point. It was as if a river of shining steel flowed leisurely and terribly past the walls of Vienna.

The Akinji, who ordinarily formed the vanguard of the host, had swept on, but in their place rode the Tatars of Crimea, crouching on their high-peaked, short-stirruped saddles, their gnome-like heads guarded by iron helmets, their stocky bodies with bronze breastplates and lacquered leather. Behind them came the Azabs, the irregular infantry, Kurds and Arabs for the most part, a wild, motley horde. Then their brothers, the Delis, the Madcaps, wild men on tough ponies fantastically adorned with fur and feathers. The riders wore caps and mantles of leopard skin; their unshorn hair hung in tangled strands about their high shoulders, and over their matted beards their eyes glared the madness of fanaticism and bhang.

After them came the real body of the army. First the beys and emirs with their retainers--horsemen and footmen from the feudal fiefs of Asia Minor. Then the Spahis, the heavy cavalry, on splendid steeds. And last of all the real strength of the Turkish empire--the most terrible military organization in the world--the Janizaries. On the walls men spat in black fury, recognizing kindred blood. For the Janizaries were not Turks. With a few exceptions, where Turkish parents had smuggled their offspring into the ranks to save them from the grinding life of a peasant, they were sons of Christians--Greeks, Serbs, Hungarians--stolen in infancy and raised in the ranks of Islam, knowing but one master--the Sultan; but one occupation--slaughter.

Their beardless features contrasted with those of their Oriental masters. Many had blue eyes and yellow mustaches. But all their faces were stamped with the wolfish ferocity to which they had been reared. Under their dark blue cloaks glinted fine mail, and many wore steel skull-caps under their curious, high-peaked hats from which depended a white sleeve-like piece of cloth, and through which was thrust a copper spoon. Long bird-of-paradise plumes likewise adorned these strange head-pieces.

Besides scimitars, pistols and daggers, each Janizary bore a matchlock, and their officers carried pots of coals for the lighting of the matches. Up and down the ranks scurried the dervishes, clad only in kalpaks of camel-hair and green aprons fringed with ebony beads, exhorting the Faithful. Military bands, the invention of the Turk, marched with the columns, cymbals clashing, lutes twanging. Over the flowing sea the banners tossed and swayed--the crimson flag of the

Spahis, the white banner of the Janizaries with its two-edged sword worked in gold, and the horse-tail standards of the rulers--seven tails for the Sultan, six for the Grand Vizier, three for the Agha of the Janizaries. So Suleyman paraded his power before despairing Caphar eyes.

But von Kalmbach's gaze was centered on the groups that labored to set up the ordnance of the Sultan. And he shook his head in bewilderment.

"Demi-culverins, sakers, and falconets!" he grunted. "Where the devil's all the heavy artillery Suleyman's so proud of?"

"At the bottom of the Danube!" A Hungarian pikeman grinned fiercely and spat as he answered. "Wulf Hagen sank that part of the Soldan's flotilla. The rest of his cannon and cannon royal, they say, were mired because of the rains."

A slow grin bristled Gottfried's mustache.

"What was Suleyman's word to Salm?"

"That he'd eat breakfast in Vienna day after tomorrow--the 29th."

Gottfried shook his head ponderously.

CHAPTER 4

The siege commenced, with the roaring of cannons, the whistling of arrows, and the blasting crash of matchlocks. The Janizaries took possession of the ruined suburbs, where fragments of walls gave them shelter. Under a screen of irregulars and a volley of arrow-fire, they advanced methodically just after dawn.

On a gun-turret on the threatened wall, leaning on his great sword and meditatively twisting his mustache, Gottfried von Kalmbach watched a Transylvanian gunner being carried off the wall, his brains oozing from a hole in his head; a Turkish matchlock had spoken too near the walls. The field-pieces of the Sultan were barking like deep-toned dogs, knocking chips off the battlements. The Janizaries were advancing, kneeling, firing, reloading as they came on. Bullets glanced from the crenelles and whined off venomously into space. One flattened against Gottfried's hauberk, bringing an outraged grunt from him. Turning toward the abandoned gun, he saw a colorful, incongruous figure bending over the massive breech.

It was a woman, dressed as von Kalmbach had not seen even the dandies of France dressed. She was tall, splendidly shaped, but lithe. From under a steel cap escaped rebellious tresses that rippled red gold in the sun over her compact shoulders. High boots of Cordovan leather came to her mid-thighs, which were cased in baggy breeches. She wore a shirt of fine Turkish mesh-mail tucked into her breeches. Her supple waist was confined by a flowing sash of green silk, into which were thrust a brace of pistols and a dagger, and from which depended a long Hungarian saber. Over all was carelessly thrown a scarlet cloak.

This surprizing figure was bending over the cannon, sighting it in a manner betokening more than a passing familiarity, at a group of Turks who were wheeling a carriage-gun just within range.

"Eh, Red Sonya!" shouted a man-at-arms, waving his pike. "Give 'em hell, my lass!"

"Trust me, dog-brother," she retorted as she applied the glowing match to the vent. "But I wish my mark was Roxelana's--"

A terrific detonation drowned her words and a swirl of smoke blinded every one on the turret, as the terrific recoil of the overcharged cannon knocked the firer flat on her back. She sprang up like a spring rebounding and rushed to the embrasure, peering eagerly through the smoke, which clearing, showed the ruin of the gun crew. The huge ball, bigger than a man's head, had smashed full into the group clustered about the saker, and now they lay on the torn ground, their skulls blasted by the impact, or their bodies mangled by the flying iron splinters from their shattered gun. A cheer went up from the towers, and the woman called Red Sonya yelled with a sincere joy and did the steps of a Cossack dance.

Gottfried approached, eying in open admiration the splendid swell of her bosom beneath the pliant mail, the curves of her ample hips and rounded limbs. She stood as a man might stand, booted legs braced wide apart, thumbs hooked into her girdle, but she was all woman. She was laughing as she faced him, and he noted with fascination the dancing sparkling lights and changing colors of her eyes. She raked back her rebellious locks with a powder-stained hand and he wondered at the clear pinky whiteness of her firm flesh where it was unstained.

"Why did you wish for the Sultana Roxelana for a target, my girl?" he asked.

"Because she's my sister, the slut!" answered Sonya.

At that instant a great cry thundered over the walls and the girl started like a wild thing, ripping out her blade in a long flash of silver in the sun.

"That bellow!" she cried. "The Janizaries--"

Gottfried was already on his way to the embrasures. He too had heard before the terrible soul-shaking shout of the charging Janizaries. Suleyman meant to waste no time on the city that barred him from helpless Europe. He meant to crush its frail walls in one storm. The bashi-bazouki, the irregulars, died like flies to screen the main advance, and over heaps of their dead, the Janizaries thundered against Vienna. In the teeth of cannonade and musket volley they surged on, crossing the moats on scaling-ladders laid across, bridge-like. Whole ranks went down as the Austrian guns roared, but now the attackers were under the walls and the cumbrous balls whirred over their heads, to work havoc in the rear ranks.

The Spanish matchlock men, firing almost straight down, took ghastly toll, but now the ladders gripped the walls, and the chanting madmen surged upward. Arrows whistled, striking down the defenders. Behind them the Turkish field-pieces boomed, careless of injury to friend as well as foe. Gottfried, standing at an embrasure, was overthrown by a sudden terrific impact. A ball had smashed the merlon, braining half a dozen defenders.

Gottfried rose, half-stunned, out of the debris of masonry and huddled corpses. He looked down into an uprushing waste of snarling, impassioned faces, where eyes glared like mad dogs' and blades glittered like sunbeams on water. Bracing his feet wide, he heaved up his great sword and lashed down. His jaw jutted out, his mustache bristled. The five-foot blade caved in steel caps and skulls, lashing through uplifted bucklers and iron shoulder-pieces. Men fell from the ladders, their nerveless fingers slipping from the bloody rungs.

But they swarmed through the breach on either side of him. A terrible cry announced that the Turks had a foothold on the wall. But no man dared leave his post to go to the threatened point. To the dazed defenders it seemed that Vienna was ringed by a glittering, tossing sea that roared higher and higher about the doomed walls.

Stepping back to avoid being hemmed in, Gottfried grunted and lashed right and left. His eyes were no longer cloudy; they blazed like blue balefire. Three Janizaries were down at his feet; his broadsword clanged in a forest of slashing scimitars. A blade splintered on his basinet, filling his eyes with fire-shot blackness. Staggering, he struck back and felt his great blade crunch home. Blood jetted over his hands and he tore his sword clear. Then with a yell and a rush someone was at his side and he heard the quick splintering of mail beneath the madly flailing strokes of a saber that flashed like silver lightning before his clearing sight.

It was Red Sonya who had come to his aid, and her onslaught was no less terrible than that of a she-panther. Her strokes followed each other too quickly for the eye to follow; her blade was a blur of white fire, and men went down like ripe grain before the reaper. With a deep roar Gottfried strode to her side, bloody and terrible, swinging his great blade. Forced irresistibly back, the Moslems wavered on the edge of the wall, then leaped for the ladders or fell screaming through empty space.

Oaths flowed in a steady stream from Sonya's red lips and she laughed wildly as her saber sang home and blood spurted along the edge. The last Turk on the battlement screamed and parried wildly as she pressed him; then dropping his scimitar, his clutching hands closed desperately on her dripping blade. With a groan he swayed on the edge, blood gushing from his horribly cut fingers.

"Hell to you, dog-soul!" she laughed. "The devil can stir your broth for you!"

With a twist and a wrench she tore away her saber, severing the wretch's fingers; with a moaning cry he pitched backward and fell headlong.

On all sides the Janizaries were falling back. The field-pieces, halted while the fighting went on upon the walls, were booming again, and the Spaniards, kneeling at the embrasures, were returning the fire with their long matchlocks.

Gottfried approached Red Sonya, who was cleansing her blade, swearing softly.

"By God, my girl," said he, extending a huge hand, "had you not come to my aid, I think I'd have supped in Hell this night. I thank--"

"Thank the devil!" retorted Sonya rudely, slapping his hand aside. "The Turks were on the wall. Don't think I risked my hide to save yours, dog-brother!"

And with a scornful flirt of her wide coattails, she swaggered off down the battlements, giving back promptly and profanely the rude sallies of the soldiers. Gottfried scowled after her, and a Lanzknecht slapped him jovially on the shoulder.

"Eh, she's a devil, that one! She drinks the strongest head under the table and outswears a Spaniard. She's no man's light o' love. Cut--slash--death to you, dog-soul! There's her way."

"Who is she, in the devil's name?" growled von Kalmbach.

"Red Sonya from Rogatino--that's all we know. Marches and fights like a man--God knows why. Swears she's sister to Roxelana, the Soldan's favorite. If the Tatars who grabbed Roxelana that night had got Sonya, by Saint Piotr! Suleyman would have had a handful! Let her alone, sir brother; she's a wildcat. Come and have a tankard of ale."

The Janizaries, summoned before the Grand Vizier to explain why the attack failed after the wall had been scaled at one place, swore they had been confronted by a devil in the form of a red-headed woman, aided by a giant in rusty mail. Ibrahim discounted the woman, but the description of the man woke a half-forgotten memory in his mind. After dismissing the soldiers, he summoned the Tatar, Yaruk Khan, and dispatched him up-country to demand of Mikhal Oglu why he had not sent a certain head to the royal tent.

CHAPTER 5

Suleyman did not eat his breakfast in Vienna on the morning of the 29th. He stood on the height of Semmering, before his rich pavilion with its gold-knobbed pinnacles and its guard of five hundred Solaks, and watched his light batteries pecking away vainly at the frail walls; he saw his irregulars wasting their lives like water, striving to fill the fosse, and he saw his sappers burrowing like moles, driving mines and counter-mines nearer and nearer the bastions.

Within the city there was little ease. Night and day the walls were manned. In their cellars the Viennese watched the faint vibrations of peas on drumheads that betrayed the sounds of digging in the earth. They told of Turkish mines burrowing under the walls, and sank their counter-mines, accordingly. Men fought no less fiercely under the earth than above.

Vienna was the one Christian island in a sea of infidels. Night by night men watched the horizons burning where the Akinji yet scoured the agonized land. Occasionally word came from the outer world--slaves escaping from the camp to slipping into the city. Always their news was fresh horror. In Upper Austria less than a third of the inhabitants were left alive; Mikhal Oglu was outdoing himself. And the people said that it was evident the vulture-winged one was looking for one in particular. His slayers brought men's heads and heaped them high before him; he avidly searched among the grisly relics, then, apparently in fiendish disappointment, drove his devils to new atrocities.

These tales, instead of paralyzing the Austrians with dread, fired them with the mad fury of desperation. Mines exploded, breaches were made and the Turks swarmed in, but always the desperate Christians were there before them, and in the choking, blind, wild-beast madness of hand-to-hand fighting they paid in part the red debt they owed.

September dwindled into October; the leaves turned brown and yellow on Wiener Wald, and the winds blew cold. The watchers shivered at night on the walls that whitened to the bite of the frost; but still the tents ringed the city; and still Suleyman sat in his magnificent pavilion and glared at the frail barrier that barred his imperial path. None but Ibrahim dared speak to him; his mood was black as the cold nights that crept down from the northern hills. The wind that moaned outside his tent seemed a dirge for his ambitions of conquest.

Ibrahim watched him narrowly, and after a vain onset that lasted from dawn till midday, he called off the Janizaries and bade them retire into the ruined suburbs and rest. And he sent a bowman to shoot a very certain shaft into a very certain part of the city, where certain persons were waiting for just such an event.

No more attacks were made that day. The field-pieces, which had been pounding at the Karnthner Gate for days, were shifted northward, to hammer at the Burg. As an assault on that part of the wall seemed imminent, the bulk of the soldiery was shifted there. But the onslaught did not come, though the batteries kept up a steady fire, hour after hour. Whatever the reason, the soldiers gave thanks for the respite; they were dizzy with fatigue, mad with raw wounds and lack of sleep.

That night the great square, the Am-Hof market, seethed with soldiers, while civilians looked on enviously. A great store of wine had been discovered hidden in the cellars of a rich Jewish merchant, who hoped to reap triple profit when all other liquor in the city was gone. In spite of their officers, the half-crazed men rolled the great hogsheads into the square and broached them. Salm gave up the attempt to control them. Better drunkenness, growled the old warhorse, than for the men to fall in their tracks from exhaustion. He paid the Jew from his own purse. In relays the soldiers came from the walls and drank deep.

In the glare of cressets and torches, to the accompaniment of drunken shouts and songs, to which the occasional rumble of a cannon played a sinister undertone, von Kalmbach dipped his basinet into a barrel and brought it out brimful and dripping. Sinking his mustache into the liquid, he paused as his clouded eyes, over the rim of the steel cap, rested on a strutting figure on the other side of the hogshead. Resentment touched his expression. Red Sonya had already visited more than one barrel. Her burganet was thrust sidewise on her rebellious locks, her swagger was wilder, her eyes more mocking.

"Ha!" she cried scornfully. "It's the Turk-killer, with his nose deep in the keg, as usual! Devil bite all topers!"

She consistently thrust a jeweled goblet into the crimson flood and emptied it at a gulp. Gottfried stiffened resentfully. He had had a tilt with Sonya already, and he still smarted.

"Why should I even look at you, in your ragged harness and empty purse," she had mocked, "when even Paul Bakics is mad for me? Go along, guzzler, beer-keg!"

"Be damned to you," he had retorted. "You needn't be so high, just because your sister is the Soldan's mistress--"

At that she had flown into an awful passion, and they had parted with mutual curses. Now, from the devil in her eyes, he saw that she intended making things further uncomfortable for him.

"Hussy!" he growled. "I'll drown you in this hogshead."

"Nay, you'll drown yourself first, boar-pig!" she shouted amid a roar of rough laughter. "A pity you aren't as valiant against the Turks as you are against the wine-butts!"

"Dogs bite you, slut!" he roared. "How can I break their heads when they stand off and pound us with cannon balls? Shall I throw my dagger at them from the wall?"

"There are thousands just outside," she retorted in the madness induced by drink and her own wild nature, "if any had the guts to go to them."

"By God!" the maddened giant dragged out his great sword. "No baggage can call me coward, sot or not! I'll go out upon them, if never a man follow me!"

Bedlam followed his bellow; the drunken temper of the crowd was fit for such madness. The nearly empty hogsheads were deserted as men tipsily drew sword and reeled toward the outer gates. Wulf Hagen fought his way into the storm, buffeting men right and left, shouting fiercely, "Wait, you drunken fools! Don't surge out in this shape! Wait--" They brushed him aside, sweeping on in a blind senseless torrent.

Dawn was just beginning to tip the eastern hills. Somewhere in the strangely silent Turkish camp a drum began to throb. Turkish sentries stared wildly and loosed their matchlocks in the air to warn the camp, appalled at the sight of the Christian horde pouring over the narrow drawbridge, eight thousand strong, brandishing swords and ale tankards. As they foamed over the moat a terrific explosion rent the din, and a portion of the wall near the Karnthner Gate seemed to detach itself and rise into the air.

A great shout rose from the Turkish camp, but the attackers did not pause.

They rushed headlong into the suburbs, and there they saw the Janizaries, not rousing from slumber, but fully clad and armed, being hurriedly drawn up in charging lines. Without pausing, they burst headlong into the half-formed ranks. Far outnumbered, their drunken fury and velocity was yet irresistible. Before the madly thrashing axes and lashing broadswords, the Janizaries reeled back dazed and disordered. The suburbs became a shambles where battling men, slashing and hewing at one another, stumbled on mangled bodies and severed limbs. Suleyman and Ibrahim, on the height of Semmering, saw the invincible Janizaries in full retreat, streaming out toward the hills.

In the city the rest of the defenders were working madly to repair the great breach the mysterious explosion had torn in the wall. Salm gave thanks for that drunken sortie. But for it, the Janizaries would have been pouring through the breach before the dust settled.

All was confusion in the Turkish camp. Suleyman ran to his horse and took charge in person, shouting at the Spahis. They formed ranks and swung down the slopes in orderly squadrons. The Christian warriors, still following their fleeing enemies, suddenly awakened to their danger. Before them the Janizaries were still falling back, but on either flank the horsemen of Asia were galloping to cut them off. Fear replaced drunken recklessness. They began to fall back, and the retreat quickly became a rout. Screaming in blind panic they threw away their weapons and fled for the drawbridge. The Turks rode them down to the water's edge, and tried to follow them across the bridge, into the gates which were opened for them. And there at the bridge Wulf Hagen and his retainers met the pursuers and held them hard. The flood of the fugitives flowed past him to safety; on him the Turkish tide broke like a red wave. He loomed, a steel-clad giant, in a waste of spears.

Gottfried von Kalmbach did not voluntarily quit the field, but the rush of his companions swept him along the tide of flight, blaspheming bitterly. Presently he lost his footing and his panic-stricken comrades stampeded across his prostrate frame. When the frantic heels ceased to drum on his mail, he raised his head and saw that he was near the fosse, and naught but Turks about him. Rising, he ran lumberingly toward the moat, into which he plunged unexpectedly, looking back over his shoulder at a pursuing Moslem.

He came up floundering and spluttering, and made for the opposite bank, splashing water like a buffalo. The blood-mad Muhammadan was close behind him--an Algerian corsair, as much at home in water as out. The stubborn German would not drop his great sword, and burdened by his mail, just managed to reach the other bank, where he

44

clung, utterly exhausted and unable to lift a hand in defense as the Algerian swirled in, dagger gleaming above his naked shoulder. Then someone swore heartily on the bank hard by. A slim hand thrust a long pistol into the Algerian's face; he screamed as it exploded, making a ghastly ruin of his head. Another slim, strong hand gripped the sinking German by the scruff of his mail.

"Grab the bank, fool!" gritted a voice, indicative of great effort. "I can't heave you up alone; you must weigh a ton. Pull, dolt, pull!"

Blowing, gasping and floundering, Gottfried half-clambered, was half lifted, out of the moat. He showed some disposition to lie on his belly and retch, what of the dirty water he had swallowed, but his rescuer urged him to his feet.

"The Turks are crossing the bridge and the lads are closing the gates against them--haste, before we're cut off."

Inside the gate Gottfried stared about, as if waking from a dream.

"Where's Wulf Hagen? I saw him holding the bridge."

"Lying dead among twenty dead Turks," answered Red Sonya.

Gottfried sat down on a piece of fallen wall, and because he was shaken and exhausted, and still mazed with drink and blood-lust, he sank his face in his huge hands and wept. Sonya kicked him disgustedly.

"Name o' Satan, man, don't sit and blubber like a spanked schoolgirl. You drunkards had to play the fool, but that can't be mended. Come--let's go to the Walloon's tavern and drink ale."

"Why did you pull me out of the moat?" he asked.

"Because a great oaf like you never can help himself. I see you need a wise person like me to keep life in that hulking frame."

"But I thought you despised me!"

"Well, a woman can change her mind, can't she?" she snapped.

Along the walls the pikemen were repelling the frothing Moslems, thrusting them off the partly repaired breach. In the royal pavilion Ibrahim was explaining to his master that the devil had undoubtedly inspired that drunken sortie just at the right moment to spoil the Grand Vizier's carefully laid plans. Suleyman, wild with fury, spoke shortly to his friend for the first time.

"Nay, thou hast failed. Have done with thine intrigues. Where craft has failed, sheer force shall prevail. Send a rider for the Akinji; they are needed here to replace the fallen. Bid the hosts to the attack again."

CHAPTER 6

The preceding onslaughts were naught to the storm that now burst on Vienna's reeling walls. Night and day the cannons flashed and thundered. Bombs burst on roofs and in the streets. When men died on the walls there was none to take their places. Fear of famine stalked the streets and the darker fear of treachery ran black-mantled through the alleys. Investigation showed that the blast that had rent the Karnthner wall had not been fired from without. In a mine tunneled from an unsuspected cellar inside the city, a heavy charge of powder had been exploded beneath the wall. One or two men, working secretly, might have done it. It was now apparent that the bombardment of the Burg had been merely a gesture to draw attention away from the Karnthner wall, to give the traitors an opportunity to work undiscovered.

Count Salm and his aides did the work of giants. The aged commander, fired with superhuman energy, trod the walls, braced the faltering, aided the wounded, fought in the breaches side by side with the common soldiers, while death dealt his blows unsparingly.

But if death supped within the walls, he feasted full without. Suleyman drove his men as relentlessly as if he were their worst foe. Plague stalked among them, and the ravaged countryside yielded no food. The cold winds howled down from the Carpathians and the warriors shivered in their light Oriental garb. In the frosty nights the hands of the sentries froze to their matchlocks. The ground grew hard as flint and the sappers toiled feebly with blunted tools. Rain fell, mingled with sleet, extinguishing matches, wetting powder, turning the plain outside the city to a muddy wallow, where rotting corpses sickened the living.

Suleyman shuddered as with an ague, as he looked out over the camp. He saw his warriors, worn and haggard, toiling in the muddy plain like ghosts under the gloomy leaden skies. The stench of his slaughtered thousands was in his nostrils. In that instant it seemed to the Sultan that he looked on a gray plain of the dead, where corpses dragged their lifeless bodies to an outworn task, animated only by the ruthless will of their master. For an instant the Tatar in his veins rose above the Turk and he shook with fear. Then his lean jaws set. The walls of Vienna staggered drunkenly, patched and repaired in a score of places. How could they stand?

"Sound for the onslaught. Thirty thousand aspers to the first man on the walls!"

The Grand Vizier spread his hands helplessly. "The spirit is gone out of the warriors. They can not endure the miseries of this icy land."

"Drive them to the walls with whips," answered Suleyman, grimly. "This is the gate to Frankistan. It is through it we must ride the road to empire."

Drums thundered through the camp. The weary defenders of Christendom rose up and gripped their weapons, electrified by the instinctive knowledge that the death-grip had come.

In the teeth of roaring matchlocks and swinging broadswords, the officers of the Sultan drove the Moslem hosts. Whips cracked and men cried out blasphemously up and down the lines. Maddened, they hurled themselves at the reeling walls, riddled with great breaches, yet still barriers behind which desperate men could crouch. Charge after charge rolled on over the choked fosse, broke on the staggering walls, and rolled back, leaving its wash of dead. Night fell unheeded, and through the darkness, lighted by blaze of cannon and flare of torches, the battle raged. Driven by Suleyman's terrible will, the attackers fought throughout the night, heedless of all Moslem tradition.

Dawn rose as on Armageddon. Before the walls of Vienna lay a vast carpet of steel-clad dead. Their plumes waved in the wind. And across the corpses staggered the hollow-eyed attackers to grapple with the dazed defenders.

The steel tides rolled and broke, and rolled on again, till the very gods must have stood aghast at the giant capacity of men for suffering and enduring. It was the Armageddon of races--Asia against Europe. About the walls raved a sea of Eastern faces--Turks, Tatars, Kurds, Arabs, Algerians, snarling, screaming, dying before the roaring matchlocks of the Spaniards, the thrust of Austrian pikes, the strokes of the German Lanzknechts, who swung their two-handed swords like reapers mowing ripe grain. Those within the walls were no more heroic than those without, stumbling among fields of their own dead.

To Gottfried von Kalmbach, life had faded to a single meaning--the swinging of his great sword. In the wide breach by the Karnthner Tower he fought until time lost all meaning. For long ages maddened faces rose snarling before him, the faces of devils, and scimitars flashed before his eyes everlastingly. He did not feel his wounds, nor the drain of weariness. Gasping in the choking dust, blind with sweat and blood, he dealt death like a harvest, dimly aware that at his side a slim, pantherish figure swayed and smote--at first with laughter, curses and snatches of song, later in grim silence.

His identity as an individual was lost in that cataclysm of swords. He hardly knew it when Count Salm was death-stricken at his side by a bursting bomb. He was not aware when night crept over the hills, nor did he realize at last that the tide was slackening and ebbing. He was only dimly aware that Nikolas Zrinyi tore him away from the corpse-choked breach, saying, "God's name, man, go and sleep. We've beaten them off--for the time being, at least."

He found himself in a narrow, winding street, all dark and forsaken. He had no idea of how he had got there, but seemed vaguely to remember a hand on his elbow, tugging, guiding. The weight of his mail pulled at his sagging shoulders. He could not tell if the sound he heard were the cannon fitfully roaring, or a throbbing in his own head. It seemed there was someone he should look for--someone who meant a great deal to him. But all was vague. Somewhere, sometime, it seemed long, long ago, a sword-stroke had cleft his basinet. When he tried to think he seemed to feel again the impact of that terrible blow, and his brain swam. He tore off the dented head-piece and cast it into the street.

Again the hand was tugging at his arm. A voice urged, "Wine, my lord--drink!"

Dimly he saw a lean, black-mailed figure extending a tankard. With a gasp he caught at it and thrust his muzzle into the stinging liquor, gulping like a man dying of thirst. Then something burst in his brain. The night filled with a million flashing sparks, as if a powder magazine had exploded in his head. After that, darkness and oblivion.

He came slowly to himself, aware of a raging thirst, an aching head, and an intense weariness that seemed to paralyze his limbs. He was bound hand and foot, and gagged. Twisting his head, he saw that he was in a small bare dusty room, from which a winding stone stair led up. He deduced that he was in the lower part of the tower.

Over a guttering candle on a crude table stooped two men. They were both lean and hook-nosed, clad in plain black garments--Asiatics, past doubt. Gottfried listened to their low-toned conversation. He had picked up many languages in his wanderings. He recognized them--Tshoruk and his son Rhupen, Armenian merchants. He remembered that he had seen Tshoruk often in the last week or so, ever since the domed helmets of the Akinji had appeared in Suleyman's camp. Evidently the merchant had been shadowing him, for some reason. Tshoruk was reading what he had written on a bit of parchment.

"My lord, though I blew up the Karnthner wall in vain, yet I have news to make my lord's heart glad. My son and I have taken the German, von Kalmbach. As he left the wall, dazed with fighting, we followed, guiding him subtly to the ruined tower whereof you know, and giving him drugged wine, bound him fast. Let my lord send the emir Mikhal Oglu to the wall by the tower, and we will give him into thy hands. We will bind him on the old mangonel and cast him over the wall like a tree trunk."

The Armenian took up an arrow and began to bind the parchment about the shaft with light silver wire.

"Take this to the roof, and shoot it toward the mantlet, as usual," he began, when Rhupen exclaimed, "Hark!" and

both froze, their eyes glittering like those of trapped vermin-
-fearful yet vindictive.

Gottfried gnawed at the gag; it slipped. Outside he heard
a familiar voice. "Gottfried! Where the devil are you?"

His breath burst from him in a stentorian roar. "Hey,
Sonya! Name of the devil! Be careful, girl--"

Tshoruk snarled like a wolf and struck him savagely on
the head with a scimitar hilt. Almost instantly, it seemed,
the door crashed inward. As in a dream Gottfried saw Red
Sonya framed in the doorway, pistol in hand. Her face was
drawn and haggard; her eyes burned like coals. Her basinet
was gone, and her scarlet cloak. Her mail was hacked and
red-clotted, her boots slashed, her silken breeches splashed
and spotted with blood.

With a croaking cry Tshoruk ran at her, scimitar lifted.
Before he could strike, she crashed down the barrel of the
empty pistol on his head, felling him like an ox. From the
other side Rhupen slashed at her with a curved Turkish
dagger. Dropping the pistol, she closed with the young
Oriental. Moving like someone in a dream, she bore him
irresistibly backward, one hand gripping his wrist, the other
his throat. Throttling him slowly, she inexorably crashed his
head again and again against the stones of the wall, until his
eyes rolled up and set. Then she threw him from her like a
sack of loose salt.

"God!" she muttered thickly, reeling an instant in the center of the room, her hands to her head. Then she went to the captive and sinking stiffly to her knees, cut his bonds with fumbling strokes that sliced his flesh as well as the cords.

"How did you find me?" he asked stupidly, clambering stiffly up.

She reeled to the table and sank down in a chair. A flagon of wine stood at her elbow and she seized it avidly and drank. Then she wiped her mouth on her sleeve and surveyed him wearily but with renewed life.

"I saw you leave the wall and followed. I was so drunk from the fighting I scarce knew what I did. I saw those dogs take your arm and lead you into the alleys, and then I lost sight of you. But I found your burganet lying outside in the street, and began shouting for you. What the hell's the meaning of this?"

She picked up the arrow, and blinked at the parchment fastened to it. Evidently she could read the Turkish characters, but she scanned it half a dozen times before the meaning became apparent to her exhaustion-numbed brain. Then her eyes flickered dangerously to the men on the floor. Tshoruk sat up, dazedly feeling the gash in his scalp; Rhupen lay retching and gurgling on the floor.

"Tie them up, brother," she ordered, and Gottfried obeyed. The victims eyed the woman much more apprehensively than him.

"This missive is addressed to Ibrahim, the Wezir," she said abruptly. "Why does he want Gottfried's head?"

"Because of a wound he gave the Sultan at Mohacz," muttered Tshoruk uneasily.

"And you, you lower-than-a-dog," she smiled mirthlessly, "you fired the mine by the Karnthner! You and your spawn are the traitors among us." She drew and primed a pistol. "When Zrinyi learns of you," she said, "your end will be neither quick nor sweet. But first, you old swine, I'm going to give myself the pleasure of blowing out your cub's brains before your eyes--"

The older Armenian gave a choking cry. "God of my fathers, have mercy! Kill me--torture me--but spare my son!"

At that instant a new sound split the unnatural quiet--a great peal of bells shattered the air.

"What's this?" roared Gottfried, groping wildly at his empty scabbard.

"The bells of Saint Stephen!" cried Sonya. "They peal for victory!"

She sprang for the sagging stair and he followed her up the perilous way. They came out on a sagging shattered roof, on a firmer part of which stood an ancient stone-casting machine, relic of an earlier age, and evidently recently repaired. The tower overlooked an angle of the wall, at which there were no watchers. A section of the ancient glacis, and a ditch interior the main moat, coupled with a steep natural pitch of the earth beyond, made the point practically invulnerable. The spies had been able to exchange messages here with little fear of discovery, and it was easy to guess the method used. Down the slope, just within long arrow-shot, stood up a huge mantlet of bullhide stretched on a wooden frame, as if abandoned there by chance. Gottfried knew that message-laden arrows were loosed from the tower roof into this mantlet. But just then he gave little thought to that. His attention was riveted on the Turkish camp. There a leaping glare paled the spreading dawn; above the mad clangor of the bells rose the crackle of flames, mingled with awful screams.

"The Janizaries are burning their prisoners," said Red Sonya.

"Judgment Day in the morning," muttered Gottfried, awed at the sight that met his eyes.

From their eyrie the companions could see almost all of the plain. Under a cold gray leaden sky, tinged a somber crimson with dawn, it lay strewn with Turkish corpses as far as the sight would carry. And the hosts of the living were melting away. From Semmering the great pavilion had vanished. The other tents were now coming down fast. Already the head of the long column was out of sight, moving into the hills through the cold dawn. Snow began falling in light swift flakes.

The Janizaries were glutting their mad disappointment on their helpless captives, hurling men, women and children living into the flames they had kindled under the somber eyes of their master, the monarch men called the Magnificent, the Merciful. All the time the bells of Vienna clanged and thundered as if their bronze throats would burst.

"They shot their bolt last night," said Red Sonya. "I saw their officers lashing them, and heard them cry out in fear beneath our swords. Flesh and blood could stand no more. Look!" She clutched her companion's arm. "The Akinji will form the rear-guard."

Even at that distance they made out a pair of vulture wings moving among the dark masses; the sullen light glimmered on a jeweled helmet. Sonya's powder-stained hands clenched so that the pink, broken nails bit into the white palms, and she spat out a Cossack curse that burned like vitriol.

"There he goes, the bastard that made Austria a desert! How easily the souls of the butchered folk ride on his cursed winged shoulders! Anyway, old warhorse, he didn't get your head."

"While he lives it'll ride loose on my shoulders," rumbled the giant.

Red Sonya's keen eyes narrowed suddenly. Seizing Gottfried's arm, she hurried downstairs. They did not see Nikolas Zrinyi and Paul Bakics ride out of the gates with their tattered retainers, risking their lives in sorties to rescue prisoners. Steel clashed along the line of march, and the Akinji retreated slowly, fighting a good rear-guard action, balking the headlong courage of the attackers by their very numbers. Safe in the depths of his horsemen, Mikhal Oglu grinned sardonically. But Suleyman, riding in the main column, did not grin. His face was like a death-mask.

Back in the ruined tower, Red Sonya propped one booted foot on a chair, and cupping her chin in her hand, stared into the fear-dulled eyes of Tshoruk.

"What will you give for your life?"

The Armenian made no reply.

"What will you give for the life of your whelp?"

The Armenian started as if stung. "Spare my son, princess," he groaned. "Anything--I will pay--I will do anything."

She threw a shapely booted leg across the chair and sat down.

"I want you to bear a message to a man."

"What man?"

"Mikhal Oglu."

He shuddered and moistened his lips with his tongue.

"Instruct me; I obey," he whispered.

"Good. We'll free you and give you a horse. Your son shall remain here as hostage. If you fail us, I'll give the cub to the Viennese to play with--"

Again the old Armenian shuddered.

"But if you play squarely, we'll let you both go free, and my pal and I will forget about this treachery. I want you to ride after Mikhal Oglu and tell him--"

Through the slush and driving snow, the Turkish column plodded slowly. Horses bent their heads to the blast; up and down the straggling lines camels groaned and complained, and oxen bellowed pitifully. Men stumbled through the mud, leaning beneath the weight of their arms and equipment. Night was falling, but no command had been given to halt. All day the retreating host had been harried by the daring Austrian cuirassiers who darted down upon them like wasps, tearing captives from their very hands.

Grimly rode Suleyman among his Solaks. He wished to put as much distance as possible between himself and the scene of his first defeat, where the rotting bodies of thirty thousand Muhammadans reminded him of his crushed ambitions. Lord of western Asia he was; master of Europe he could never be. Those despised walls had saved the Western world from Moslem dominion, and Suleyman knew it. The rolling thunder of the Ottoman power re-echoed around the world, paling the glories of Persia and Mogul India. But in the West the yellow-haired Aryan barbarian stood unshaken. It was not written that the Turk should rule beyond the Danube.

Suleyman had seen this written in blood and fire, as he stood on Semmering and saw his warriors fall back from the ramparts, despite the flailing lashes of their officers. It had been to save his authority that he gave the order to break camp--it burned his tongue like gall, but already his soldiers were burning their tents and preparing to desert him. Now in darkly brooding silence he rode, not even speaking to Ibrahim.

In his own way Mikhal Oglu shared their savage despondency. It was with a ferocious reluctance that he turned his back on the land he had ruined, as a half-glutted panther might be driven from its prey. He recalled with satisfaction the blackened, corpse-littered wastes--the screams of tortured men--the cries of girls writhing in his iron arms; recalled with much the same sensations the death-shrieks of those same girls in the blood-fouled hands of his killers.

But he was stung with the disappointment of a task undone--for which the Grand Vizier had lashed him with stinging word. He was out of favor with Ibrahim. For a lesser man that might have meant a bowstring. For him it meant that he would have to perform some prodigious feat to reinstate himself. In this mood he was dangerous and reckless as a wounded panther.

Snow fell heavily, adding to the miseries of the retreat. Wounded men fell in the mire and lay still, covered by a growing white mantle. Mikhal Oglu rode among his rearmost ranks, straining his eyes into the darkness. No foe had been sighted for hours. The victorious Austrians had ridden back to their city.

The columns were moving slowly through a ruined village, whose charred beams and crumbling fire-seared walls stood blackly in the falling snow. Word came back down the lines that the Sultan would pass on through and camp in a valley which lay a few miles beyond.

The quick drum of hoofs back along the way they had come caused the Akinji to grip their lances and glare slit-eyed into the flickering darkness. They heard but a single horse, and a voice calling the name of Mikhal Oglu. With a word the chief stayed a dozen lifted bows, and shouted in return. A tall, gray stallion loomed out of the flying snow, a black-mantled figure crouched grotesquely atop of it.

"Tshoruk! You Armenian dog! What in the name of Allah--"

The Armenian rode close to Mikhal Oglu and whispered urgently in his ear. The cold bit through the thickest garments. The Akinji noted that Tshoruk was trembling violently. His teeth chattered and he stammered in his speech. But the Turk's eyes blazed at the import of his message.

"Dog, do you lie?"

"May I rot in hell if I lie!" A strong shudder shook Tshoruk and he drew his kaftan close about him. "He fell from his horse, riding with the cuirassiers to attack the rear-guard, and lies with a broken leg in a deserted peasant's hut some three miles back--alone except for his mistress Red Sonya, and three or four Lanzknechts, who are drunk on wine they found in the deserted camp."

Mikhal Oglu wheeled his horse with sudden intent.

"Twenty men to me!" he barked. "The rest ride on with the main column. I go after a head worth its weight in gold. I'll overtake you before you go in camp."

Othman caught his jeweled rein. "Are you mad, to ride back now? The whole country will be on our heels--"

He reeled in his saddle as Mikhal Oglu slashed him across the mouth with his riding whip. The chief wheeled away, followed by the men he had designated. Like ghosts they vanished into the spectral darkness.

Othman sat his horse uncertainly, looking after them. The snow shafted down, the wind sobbed drearily among the bare branches. There was no sound except the receding noises of the trudging column. Presently these ceased. Then Othman started. Back along the way they had come, he heard a distant reverberation, a roar as of forty or fifty matchlocks speaking together. In the utter silence which followed, panic came upon Othman and his warriors. Whirling away they fled through the ruined village after the retreating horde.

CHAPTER 7

None noticed when night fell on Constantinople, for the splendor of Suleyman made night no less glorious than day. Through gardens that were riots of blossoms and perfume, cressets twinkled like myriad fireflies. Fireworks turned the city into a realm of shimmering magic, above which the minarets of five hundred mosques rose like towers of fire in an ocean of golden foam. Tribesmen on Asian hills gaped and marveled at the blaze that pulsed and glowed afar, paling the very stars. The streets of Stamboul were thronged with crowds in the attire of holiday and rejoicing. The million lights shone on jeweled turban and striped khalat--on dark eyes sparkling over filmy veils--on shining palanquins borne on the shoulders of huge ebony-skinned slaves.

All that splendor centered in the Hippodrome, where in lavish pageants the horsemen of Turkistan and Tatary competed in breathtaking races with the riders of Egypt and Arabia, where warriors in glittering mail spilled one another's blood on the sands, where swordsmen were matched against wild beasts, and lions were pitted against tigers of Bengal and boars from northern forests. One might have deemed the imperial pageantry of Rome revived in Eastern garb.

On a golden throne, set upon lapis lazuli pillars, Suleyman reclined, gazing on the splendors, as purpletogaed Caesars had gazed before him. About him bowed his viziers and officers, and the ambassadors from foreign courts--Venice, Persia, India, the khanates of Tatary. They came--including the Venetians--to congratulate him on his victory over the Austrians. For this grand fete was in celebration of that victory, as set forth in a manifesto under the Sultan's hand, which stated, in part, that the Austrians having made submission and sued for pardon on their knees, and the German realms being so distant from the Ottoman empire, "the Faithful would not trouble to clean out the fortress (Vienna), or purify, improve, and put it in repair." Therefore the Sultan had accepted the submission of the contemptible Germans, and left them in possession of their paltry "fortress"!

Suleyman was blinding the eyes of the world with the blaze of his wealth and glory, and striving to make himself believe that he had actually accomplished all he had intended. He had not been beaten on the field of open battle; he had set his puppet on the Hungarian throne; he had devastated Austria; the markets of Stamboul and Asia were full of Christian slaves. With this knowledge he soothed his vanity, ignoring the fact that thirty thousand of his subjects rotted before Vienna, and that his dreams of European conquest had been shattered.

Behind the throne shone the spoils of war--silken and velvet pavilions, wrested from the Persians, the Arabs, the Egyptian memluks; costly tapestries, heavy with gold embroidery. At his feet were heaped the gifts and tributes of subject and allied princes. There were vests of Venetian velvet, golden goblets crusted with jewels from the courts of the Grand Moghul, ermine-lined kaftans from Erzeroum, carven jade from Cathay, silver Persian helmets with horse-hair plumes, turban-cloths, cunningly sewn with gems, from Egypt, curved Damascus blades of watered steel, matchlocks from Kabul worked richly in chased silver, breastplates and shields of Indian steel, rare furs from Mongolia. The throne was flanked on either hand by a long rank of youthful slaves, made fast by golden collars to a single, long silver chain. One file was composed of young Greek and Hungarian boys, the other of girls; all clad only in plumed head-pieces and jeweled ornaments intended to emphasize their nudity.

Eunuchs in flowing robes, their rotund bellies banded by cloth-of-gold sashes, knelt and offered the royal guests sherbets in gemmed goblets, cooled with snow from the mountains of Asia Minor. The torches danced and flickered to the roars of the multitudes. Around the courses swept the horses, foam flying from their bits; wooden castles reeled and went up in flames as the Janizaries clashed in mock warfare. Officers passed among the shouting people, tossing showers of copper and silver coins amongst them. None hungered or thirsted in Stamboul that night except the miserable Caphar captives. The minds of the foreign envoys were numbed by the bursting sea of splendor, the thunder of imperial magnificence. About the vast arena stalked trained elephants, almost covered with housings of gold-worked leather, and from the jeweled towers on their backs, fanfares of trumpets vied with the roar of the throngs and the bellowing of lions. The tiers of the Hippodrome were a sea of faces, all turning toward the jeweled figure on the shining throne, while thousands of tongues wildly thundered his acclaim.

As he impressed the Venetian envoys, Suleyman knew he impressed the world. In the blaze of his magnificence, men would forget that a handful of desperate Caphars behind rotting walls had closed his road to empire. Suleyman accepted a goblet of the forbidden wine, and spoke aside to the Grand Vizier, who stepped forth and lifted his arms.

"Oh, guests of my master, the Padishah forgets not the humblest in the hour of rejoicing. To the officers who led his hosts against the infidels, he has made rare gifts. Now he gives two hundred and forty thousand ducats to be distributed among the common soldiers, and likewise to each Janizary he gives a thousand aspers."

In the midst of the roar that went up, a eunuch knelt before the Grand Vizier, holding up a large round package, carefully bound and sealed. A folded piece of parchment, held shut by a red seal, accompanied it. The attention of the Sultan was attracted.

"Oh, friend, what has thou there?"

Ibrahim salaamed. "The rider of the Adrianople post delivered it, oh Lion of Islam. Apparently it is a gift of some sort from the Austrian dogs. Infidel riders, I understand, gave it into the hands of the border guard, with instructions to send it straightway to Stamboul."

"Open it," directed Suleyman, his interest roused. The eunuch salaamed to the floor, then began breaking the seals of the package. A scholarly slave opened the accompanying note and read the contents, written in a bold yet feminine hand:

To the Soldan Suleyman and his Wezir Ibrahim and to the hussy Roxelana we who sign our names below send a gift in token of our immeasurable fondness and kind affection.

Sonya of Rogatino, and Gottfried von Kalmbach

Suleyman, who had started up at the name of his favorite, his features suddenly darkening with wrath, gave a choking cry, which was echoed by Ibrahim. The eunuch had torn the seals of the bale, disclosing what lay within. A pungent scent of herbs and preservative spices filled the air, and the object, slipping from the horrified eunuch's hands, tumbled among the heaps of presents at Suleyman's feet, offering a ghastly contrast to the gems, gold and velvet bales. The Sultan stared down at it and in that instant his shimmering pretense of triumph slipped from him; his glory turned to tinsel and dust. Ibrahim tore at his beard with a gurgling, strangling sound, purple with rage.

At the Sultan's feet, the features frozen in a death-mask of horror, lay the severed head of Mikhal Oglu, Vulture of the Grand Turk.

www.ingramcontent.com/pod-product-compliance
Lightning Source LLC
Chambersburg PA
CBHW030239180626
46810CB00008B/3202